Changes

Changes

Written By
Mahawa Bangoura

Cover Design by

Mohamed Bangoura

Artistic Rendering by

David Gonzalez

Newark, Delaware

Changes

Summary:

Front Cover Designed by: Mohamed Bangoura
Front Cover Artist Rendering by: David Gonzalez

Gladstone Publishing Services
Paperback:
ISBN-13 978-1-928681-33-5

1. School-Fiction. 2. Family-Fiction 3. Interpersonal relations -
Fiction. 4. Friendship-Fiction

Printed in the United States of America

Dedication

I dedicate this book to my family for always loving me faithfully and teaching me to believe that I can do anything I put my mind to because there are no limits to my forthcoming success. I am allowed to dream bigger than clouds I see in the sky, shine brighter than the sun outside my window, and I know that my dreams are limitless, and can become my reality. I also want to dedicate this book to my Aunt Lynn, and one of my older brothers, Khaleel. This book would not be possible without them. So a major thank you to them from the bottom of my heart.

Introduction

I was in the car coming home. My mom was driving. We had just left Grandma Lyla's house. I was six years old then. Right before I went to sleep that night, there was a huge bump! Everything went pitch black!

I felt a hand around my neck carrying me. I slightly fluttered my eyes open. Red and blue lights were everywhere, and sirens were screaming from everywhere. It felt like my ears were bleeding. I looked over to the other side of me, and someone was carrying my mother. I couldn't make out the face of the person who was carrying her. Her face didn't look damaged or anything, but her eyes were creepily open. Her arms were bleeding, and her beautiful brown hair flopped, as the guy or girl (don't know) carried her. Her neck bobbed up and down, as she was carried

"Mommy," I said and then my eyes closed. A faded voice kept calling my name.

~1~

"Alyssa? Hey, wake up!" My little brother, Cole's voice rang in my head. My eyes opened, and I gasped.

"Where's Mom?" I asked him. He looked at me and then raised his eyebrows.

"Where is she?!" I asked grabbing him by the collar.

"She's in her coffin. In the ground!" he said sarcastically while trying to get me off his collar. I let him go.

"You forgot?" he asked. I didn't say anything. He turned around and left. On his way downstairs I heard him say to himself, "Who forgets their mother is dead?"

I looked over at a picture of my mother and me. Her hair was in a messy bun. She was giving me a hug while I was facing the camera. My arms were around her neck, and I was smiling, so big. I also had two missing teeth in the front. I started to cry.

Changes

I hate the nightmares about me being in the accident that caused my mother to die.

"Alyssa?" My father's head poked in.

"Hey, you okay?" he asked me. I quickly wiped away my tears.

"Is it the nightmares again?" he said sitting down on my bed.

"Yeah," I said quietly.

"I'm sorry that you were a part of the accident, Honey, but it's over. It's been done, and you can't do anything about that. It happened five years ago," Daddy said putting his arms around me. I laid my head on his shoulder.

"C'mon, Honey, you got to get dressed for school," Daddy said leaving.

"Daddy?" I said. He turned around and looked at me waiting. "I love you," I said.

"Love you too, Allie," he smiled. I smiled as he left. I started to get ready for school.

I put on my blue jeans with my purple shirt. I gently pulled my dark brown hair into a ponytail. I got my homework, and I went downstairs.

"But, Dad, if I had a nightmare and I woke up, I would ask myself what part of that nightmare was real and what was not," I heard Cole talking to Daddy.

"But, Bud, you have to remember that Allie was a part of that accident and she has nightmares about it," Daddy said, his mouth full.

"...She forgot Mom died!" Cole screamed.

"Lower your voice, Cole," Daddy said, in a warning tone.

"One, she didn't forget, it was wishful thinking. She wants her mom back. Two, how could you not see what she is going through?"

"Because I'm not a girl!" Cole screamed. Daddy looked at him.

I came downstairs and said, "Good morning." Cole ran and hid behind Daddy.

Changes

"Please, Allie. Don't...don't grab me again. Dad already fixed my collar," he said. I rolled my eyes. My seven-year-old little brother is so not helpful!

"Leave her alone Cole," Daddy said. He turned around and said, "Ready to go? Have your homework?" I nodded yes.

"Eat up because I gotta go to work," Daddy said.

»»»»

"Bye, Daddy. Love you," I said getting out of the car. Daddy was dropping me off. He waved goodbye to me.

"Bye, Allie," Cole said from the back seat. I smiled and waved to him, happy that he had forgotten about this morning.

"Hey, Allie!" my best friend Katrina Loe said. Everyone called her Kat, though.

"Hi, Kat, what's up?" I said to her.

"Nothing really, just wanted to know what page we had for math yesterday?" she asked, her cheeks burning red. I shook my head in disappointment. Kat always forgets her homework.

"Page 463," I said to her.

"Thank you."

"You're welcome."

"Class quiet down," Mrs. Taylor said to everyone. I hate math class! It's so difficult! My mother used to help me. My dad helped too, but now not a lot because he has to grade papers and everything. My dad is a 5th-grade teacher.

"Who can do last night's homework?" she asked. Everyone raised their hand. She looked curious.

"On the board?" she asked again. A few hands went down. I didn't raise my hand at all.

"How about you Katrina?" Mrs. Taylor looked at Kat.

Kat smiled. Even though she does not do her homework, she knows how to work those problems. Kat's very smart, but she acts like she doesn't know anything. But the teachers know. Last year, in 5th grade, we were both in my dad's class, and he told her she didn't need to act like that. But I guess she didn't listen.

Changes

On the board, she knew the answer to question number nine. The teacher looked at her and then the answer. Mrs. Taylor broke into a smile.

"Beautiful work, Katrina," Mrs. Taylor praised her. Kat smiled again and then whipped her blonde hair like the cheerleader that she is. I rolled my eyes.

"Come do number ten, Alyssa," Mrs. Taylor said. I jumped at the sound of my name. Everyone looked at me.

"Me?" I said to Mrs. Taylor making sure she was talking to me. I nervously walked up to the front of the classroom. I looked and scanned my math homework for number ten. Then, I saw it. Shoot! I had problems with that problem yesterday when I was doing my homework. I wrote my answer.

"Nine?" someone called out.

"Ha! She said the answer was nine. Dumbbell or should I say, dumb girl," said the boy again. My heart started to beat fast as if I was running. Everyone laughed...including Kat. I looked at Mrs. Taylor ready to cry.

"Did you do your homework?" she asked.

"Yeah," I said.

"Hmm. Then why..."

I looked behind me. People were pointing at the board and at me. Whispering, judging, AND gossiping. With tears at the back of my eyes, I asked to use the bathroom.

"Yes, but hurry. Class is almost over," Mrs. Taylor said erasing my awfully wrong work from the board.

I dashed out of the room. No one was in the hallways. Good, because the tears spilled out very quickly. I was in the bathroom looking in the mirror. My face was now red. My green eyes looked more like seaweed green instead of emerald green.

In the mirror, for a moment, I thought I saw my mother. Like...I thought I saw her face. But that's impossible and obviously wishful thinking. I scanned the bathroom...but nothing.

"Look at you. So grown up," I heard her say. Right then I turned around, I saw her. She was in a white dress. Her brown hair was down to her elbows and her green eyes, like mine, sparkled in the middle of the school bathroom.

Changes

"Mommy!" I ran to her and I put my arms around her. She put her hands on my shoulders.

"Little girl?" she said. For some reason, her voice had changed.

"Please. Please stop hugging me...and calling me mommy," I looked up at my mother who I now saw was an 8th-grade teacher wearing a white dress. Her eyes were actually more hazel than green, and she had light brown hair. This...was apparently really embarrassing.

Hugging an 8th-grade teacher? Thinking she was my mother? In the bathroom?! Yep! Mmm, embarrassing.

"I'm so sorry. I..." I laughed. "I thought, you were someone else," I explained to her so she wouldn't think I was a nut job.

"I completely understand," said the teacher. I just stood there.

"Shouldn't you go back to class now?"

"Yeah, I should. Bye," I said even though I did not want to go back to my class. I ran to my classroom and found everyone getting ready for second period.

"Remember Alyssa you have to have page 464 done," Mrs. Taylor said. I nodded yes. I gathered my books to go to second period.

"It's okay that you got the answer wrong," Kat said to me in the hallway. I groaned under my breath. She's gonna give me the sympathy.

"I know that it's okay," I said.

"Then why did you leave?" she asked.

"I had to use the bathroom."

"Why did it take so long?"

"None of your business," I said, sick of her question and answer game. She sighed.

"I just wanted to make you feel better," she said.

"I don't need your help," I said back.

"The next time I make you feel better is never," she said and then fiercely stomped away.

When I was sure she couldn't hear me I said, "I don't think I care."

》》》》

I was waiting in the car line for Daddy to pick me up. I don't go on the bus like other people do. I used to in first to fifth grade.

"Your daddy's here, Alyssa," said Mr. Klucking Worthe. I got up and put on my bookbag. I waved goodbye to Mr. Klucking Worthe.

"How was your day?" Daddy said when I hopped in.

"Fine," I said.

"Did you have a nightmare trying to daydream in school?" Cole asked from the back seat. I looked at Daddy who gave Cole a warning look to stop it.

"You know you have to let things go. Right?" I asked.

"You don't let things go. Like when you broke my phone," Cole said.

"One, look who's talking. Two, it was a phone that only said hello and goodbye with plastic numbers on it," I pointed out.

Cole had a phone, a play phone, that wasn't even real. It was a flip phone. When you opened it, it said, "Hello." When you don't play with it or leave it alone, for like five minutes, it said, "Goodbye." I accidentally stepped on it once and he has never forgiven me. Oh, and by the way that was two years ago!

Anyway, today is Friday. So that means we're gonna go over to Grandma Lyla's house. We go visit and stay with her for the whole weekend, once a month.

I love Grandma Lyla! She is seriously the best grandma in the whole world. She's my mother's mother. Out of everyone, she was the most hurt and devastated, when my mother died. I don't even really know how to explain to you her feelings. I mean come on, Grandma Lyla has four children, and my mother was her only girl. So when my mother died, it's like a piece of Grandma Lyla died too.

If you're thinking about my grandpa...don't. Grandpa Mick died when I was two years old. There's this one picture my mother took of me sitting in Grandpa Mick's lap. Grandma Lyla lost her husband and daughter. I felt so sad for her.

Changes

"Guys, go get your stuff, and we'll go to grandma's," Daddy said when we got home. I went up to my room to pack. Grandma Lyla still had some of our old clothes there that I can wear, so I just took entertainment stuff. I brought my iPod touch, my DS, and my personal journal. I put all of it in my silver suitcase.

I walked downstairs and found Daddy texting someone. There was a huge smile on his face. Then he started to laugh.

"Daddy, you ready?" I asked. He jumped up.

"Oh...uh...yeah," he said. I smiled. Then Cole came running, with his pet lizard.

"Cole, you can't take Bitty with you," Daddy said.

"Why? Bitty will miss me, though," Cole said. Daddy sighed. He went over to Cole and took Bitty. Cole frowned.

"I want that frown off your face before we get to Grandma Lyla's," Daddy warned. I shook my head and then followed Daddy out to the car.

After a while, I drifted off to sleep. Suddenly, I felt the car had stopped.

"Why'd we stop?" I screamed. Daddy reached over to me and put his hand over mine.

"Everything's fine Honey. We're at the gas station," Daddy explained. I looked over to my right side and saw Cole sleeping. I wish I could sleep, but you know what'll happen.

"How long is it to reach Grandma Lyla's?" I asked.

Daddy squinted. "About 10 minutes if there's no traffic," he said. I sighed.

"Hey," Daddy said looking at me through the rearview mirror.

"You can go to sleep. I'll drive carefully," he said. I nodded and closed my eyes. This time, no huge bumps, no sirens, but silence. Finally, I could relax. Sweet, sweet, silence.

»»»

I heard the car door opening and closing. I opened my eyes and found Daddy getting out of the car at Grandma Lyla's house.

"Cole? Cole, wake up! We're here!" I said shaking him. He swatted at me and then opened his eyes.

"Where are we?" he asked rubbing his eyes.

"We're at Grandma Lyla's," I said to him.

"Yes! Finally!" he screamed. Then, he opened the door and went after Daddy. I wasn't just gonna sit there so I followed him.

"I missed you too, Baby," she said. Then she looked up to Daddy. He smiled at her and she smiled back. Finally, I let her go.

"Where's my grandson?" Grandma Lyla said playfully. Cole looked around like he didn't know who she was talking about.

"Oh, come here!" Grandma Lyla said reaching out to get him from Daddy. She kissed his chubby cheeks. He laughed.

"How are you, Joe?" Grandma Lyla said to Daddy, putting down Cole.

"I'm great. Just taking care of my kids," Daddy said putting his hand through his dark brown hair.

"Good. Now you can take a break from your kids. I'll take care of them," Grandma Lyla smiled. Daddy did too. Then, he went to get our stuff.

"Thank you," I said to Daddy when he gave me my suitcase.

He mouthed, "You're welcome."

I smiled. Then gave him a hug.

"Bye, Daddy," I said.

"Bye, Alyssa. Don't kill your brother," Daddy said. I laughed. He always knew how to do it. Then Cole came running.

"Bye," he said.

"Aren't you going to give me a hug, Bud?" Daddy said his hands on his hips.

"No," Cole turned around, "but, I'll give you a fist bump. Hugging is for babies," he said. Daddy looked at me.

"I guess that still continues in the second grade," I said out loud.

So, in the second grade, everyone was convinced that hugging was for babies, after watching a movie called "Hugging Is For Babies." Stupid, right? Well, that's what we thought. So, I guess they still show that movie. The "curse" wears off in third grade, so I'm not really worried about my brother...or should I be?

"So, what do you guys want to do?" Grandma Lyla asked like five minutes after Daddy left.

"I want to talk to you Grandma Lyla," I said. Cole huffed.

"Talking is boring," he said to me.

"You're boring," I said back.

"Ehh," we both said, at the same time, sticking out our tongues at each other.

"What about...we go out to dinner," Grandma Lyla said and then looked at us, "that way we can talk and do whatever Cole wants to do which right now I have no idea." Both Cole and I smiled.

"Eat-A-Lot!" We both said at the same time.

Eat-A-Lot was a restaurant close to Grandma Lyla's house. Driving, it was like 5 to 10 minutes, but longer if you wanted to walk. I loved going to Eat-A-Lot. They seriously had delicious food, but I bet Grandma Lyla could make something much better...yeah, you heard me. She was one of the best cooks. Anyway, we left to go to Eat-A-Lot.

>>>>>

"So, now I don't think Kat is going to talk to me," I explained what happened to Kat and me to Grandma Lyla.

"Oh wow... did you tell your father?" Grandma Lyla said opening the door to Eat-A-Lot. I hesitated before speaking.

"No...no, not really. I don't talk to Daddy about school unless it has to do with homework or something like that," I said. "In other words, she barely talks to Dad," Cole jumped in. I shook my head. Cole! Grandma Lyla laughed at us.

"I understand, Alyssa. If your mother was here, you would talk to her," Grandma Lyla said. I smiled. Grandma Lyla always got me. We went and sat down at a table. We hadn't been to Eat-A-Lot for a while, so it was nice to be here.

I looked around the fancy restaurant. There weren't a lot of people here since it was like 5 o'clock pm on a Friday night. Most people would come around 7 o'clock. The food here was good but it did cost a lot of money. I knew some of the waiters and waitresses here too.

"What would you like to order today Lyla?" asked a tall waitress with long red hair and green eyes. She looked familiar, to me. She was like in her thirties.

"Hello Riley," Grandma Lyla said to the women. She looked at me. "What do you want, Alyssa?" Grandma Lyla asked.

"Can I have a chicken sandwich please?" I said.

"Wait. Alyssa?" the waitress asked.

"Yeah," I said. She put down her pad and gave me a hug.

"Do you remember me? I used to babysit you. It's me, Riley," Riley said. Then a spark lit in me.

"Riley!" I hugged her back.

Riley was my mother's closest friend, and when I was like 2 or 3 years old, she used to babysit me. But, when we moved, I lost contact with Riley.

"Hi. How have you been?" she asked.

"Good," I said back. Another waitress came and whispered something to Riley. Riley's face seemed to turn a little sad.

"Sorry, I can't talk, but what would you like Lyla and…?"

"My name is Cole," Cole interrupted.

"Right, you're Kara's second one," Riley smiled. Cole smiled, relieved she at least knew something about him.

"Can I have a chicken sandwich, please, too?" Cole said. Riley smiled and looked at me.

"Like sister, like brother," Riley said.

"Oh please," I mumbled so no one could hear me.

"Lyla?" Riley said looking at Grandma Lyla.

"Can I have a salad please?" she smiled. Riley nodded her head and then left.

"That woman used to babysit you?" Cole asked.

"Yeah. Before you were born," I said. Cole glared.

"I bet she didn't like you," he said with a smirk.

"Why, do you think she'll like you even more?" I asked. His smirk fell out of place.

"Well...um...you-"

"Yeah right!" I interrupted him.

"Guys stop it. You guys should be talking about school or something," Grandma Lyla said. Cole and I both sighed.

About ten minutes later the food came. Yes! I was starving!

"Thank you, Riley," Grandma Lyla smiled. Riley smiled back and then left.

"I am hungry," I said

"Let's eat up!" Grandma Lyla said.

»»»

"Did you guys enjoy your food?" Riley asked no longer wearing her black and white uniform.

"Yes, thank you," Grandma Lyla said.

"Are you busy Riley?" I asked.

"I have a seven-year-old son that's waiting for me near your grandmother's house," Riley smiled.

"What are you trying to say, Alyssa?" Grandma Lyla asked me.

"I just want to know if Riley can come over," I said. Riley looked at Grandma Lyla.

"Of course, but this is your decision, Riley," Grandma Lyla said. I looked at Riley with hopeful eyes.

"Yeah, why not. I miss Alyssa," she decided. I smiled.

"Can your son come?" Cole asked.

"Yeah just let me call his father to bring him," Riley said. Cole smiled. I'm actually happy because then he won't be bugging me to death.

"Well, here's the check. And, we're ready to go," Grandma Lyla said. We got up and started to leave. Then a guy with blonde hair came in with a little boy (about seven years old) that also had blonde hair.

Changes

"Brady, come over here," Riley said to the boy. The boy came and gave Riley a hug. She kissed the top of his head. I guessed that was her son.

"Brady, this is Alyssa and Cole. You know Miss Lyla," Riley introduced us. I smiled when she said my name. Cole smiled when his name was called.

"Do you remember Miss Kara? The woman I always talk about?" Riley asked. Brady nodded his head, yes. "These are her children, and we're gonna be with them for a while," Cole and I smiled.

~2~

"Oh my God, you like Leonardo too?" Cole said to Brady in Grandma Lyla's family room. They had been talking about things I didn't even know about since we left Eat-A-Lot.

"So, how have you been? What's going on with you?" Riley asked. I hesitated.

"Where should I start?" I asked.

"First, what grade are you in now?" she said sipping her wine.

"I'm in 6th grade,"

"Is it rough?"

"Very. But I'm fine."

"You miss Kara...er...your mother?" Riley asked looking straight into my eyes.

"I do," I said back. Riley laughed.

"What? What happened?" I asked confused.

"Nothing. It's just that you look exactly like her when we were your age," Riley explained.

"I do?" I said shocked for some weird reason. I don't know why. I mean she was my mother. Am I not supposed to look like her? But again...I'm still shocked.

"You really do. Hasn't your grandmother showed you a picture of your mother when she was your age?" Riley asked. I shook my head no. Riley got up and went into the kitchen.

Grandma Lyla walked toward me and said, "I want to give you something." She opened the attic door. She climbed up, and I followed her. The boys came too. The attic was filled with boxes both opened and closed. It was a little junky. I bet, Grandma Lyla kept almost everything and anything up here. She opened a brown box that said, "Kara", in bright blue. That was my mother's favorite color. Grandma Lyla took a black journal from the box with white small flowers on it.

"I was looking up here the other day, and I looked in this box. I found your mother's old journals she used to keep. I thought you might want to read them," Grandma Lyla smiled. My mouth turned into a big smile.

"Thank you!" I said and then went over and gave her a hug.

"Mom never told me she had journals," I said admiring the journal.

"Maybe it was because you were five years old and was just learning to read or she forgot to tell you," Grandma Lyla said. I blushed. Cole came over and looked at it.

"Mom had a journal?" he asked. It sounded weird when Cole said, "Mom."

He was never really serious about her. I can't really blame him either. He was two years old, when she passed, so he didn't know her like I did. But, the more I grew up, her picture faded in my mind, but she'll never completely fade. I won't let that happen.

"Can I see that please?" Riley asked smiling.

"Of course," I said. Riley opened the black journal. Her eyes moved back and forth reading the journal. Then she went to the next one. Her eyes started to tear up.

"Mom?" Brady said to Riley. She covered her mouth and then the teared poured out.

"I'm so sorry," she said between sniffles.

"Let's get you cleaned up," Grandma Lyla said putting her arms around Riley. They went downstairs, Brady and Cole followed them. I sat down and opened the journal. I started to read.

Dear Journal,

Riley (my best friend) is here. We're having a sleepover. Mama actually allowed it since Riley has been gone for awhile. You will not believe what Riley just said to me. She thinks my socks reek! Maybe they do, but she didn't have to tell me. Oh, sorry but I gotta go. Bye!!!!

Kara

I laughed after reading. My mom was so goofy when she was younger. I think Riley cried because she missed her best friend. They knew each other since they were in second grade. The journal I was reading talked about when they were in 6th grade. Right when I went to read again, Cole's head popped in.

"Grandma Lyla wants you to come down to say bye to Riley," he said. I picked myself up and went downstairs.

"Bye Riley, thank you for visiting," I said.

She smiled. "Goodbye, Alyssa. Take care of yourself," Riley said and then closed the door.

Grandma Lyla looked at her watch. "It's 10 o'clock, guys. So everyone go to your rooms and do whatever. But I want lights out on the dot at 10:30," Grandma Lyla ordered.

"Yes, ma'am!" Cole and I saluted. Grandma Lyla laughed.

"You guys are adorable," Grandma Lyla said and then left the room. I started to go upstairs.

"Allie?" Cole called my name. I turned around to look at him.

"Do you want to play on the Xbox with me?" he asked. His face looked sad. No one else was gonna play with him. If we were home it would be Daddy. As much as he drove me crazy, he was still my little brother. Besides, I'll win at whatever game we play.

"Yeah...but only fifteen minutes," I said to him.

"Yes! Thank you!" he came and gave me a hug. I rolled my eyes.

"Can we go and stop wasting time?" I asked.

"Yeah, yeah, you're right," Cole said agreeing with me.

We went up to his room. The wall was a bright blue with clouds everywhere. My mother and I painted the clouds when she was pregnant with Cole. I was four so some clouds looked sloppy.

"A boxing game?" Cole asked holding up the game.

"Of course," I said. My avatar was a girl with blonde hair. Cole picked a man with scars all over his face. We started to play.

"That was a hard round," Cole said rubbing his eyes.

"You've said that since we began to play," I pointed out. He'd been losing really badly, and that's why he was complaining.

"Let's play something else," he said getting up.

"Yeah, no. I'm going in my room. We've been playing for more than fifteen minutes," I said rubbing my eyes.

"Okay. Bye," Cole said as the disc came out the Xbox.

I went into my room and closed the door. I changed into my pajamas. I took my hair out of the ponytail. I went into my personal bathroom that was connected to my room. I brushed my hair as I watched myself in the mirror. Then, I just looked at my hair. It had gotten longer. Yikes! I knew my hair grew fast, but sometimes it was scary.

Two months ago it was down to my elbows. Now it was at my hips. I remembered every night Mommy used to braid my hair before I went to bed. Now that I was eleven she would probably brush it every night...I don't know. I also don't want to think about it because it'll make me sad.

I sat on my bed. I looked at my heart shaped alarm clock. It was 10:25. I had five minutes to do something small. So I got my mom's journal.

Dear Journal,

I should be sleeping but I have to write in here. It's 10:36 PM and Riley is already knocked out. I mean I can still make it to 11:00 or maybe even 12:00. Okay, maybe not 12 because I know I'm a sleepy person. And Mama will come check on me. So um Riley and I had fun with our sleepover. Oh no! I just yawned. Okay, I'm gonna go now.

-Kara

I smiled. I looked at the time and yup, it was time. I put the journal down and turned off the lights. A few minutes later my door creaked open. Grandma Lyla's head appeared in the dark. I turned the light back on. She smiled.

"Goodnight, Alyssa," she said.

"Goodnight," I said back.

>>>>

The sun shined in my room the next day. I heard the birds tweeting outside. I took my pillow, and I put it over my face. Almost five seconds later, I got up and used the bathroom. And then, I brushed my teeth. When I was done, I went downstairs.

I found Grandma Lyla and Cole eating breakfast. Grandma Lyla's white hair was down instead of in a messy bun.

"Good morning Grandma Lyla," I said giving her a kiss.

"Hello, Alyssa. If you are hungry you can have some pancakes and eggs," Grandma Lyla said putting her plate in the sink. I looked at the pancakes and eggs she had made and my stomach growled. Oh yeah, I'm hungry. I got a plate from the cabinet. I put the pancakes and eggs on my plate and sat down. Cole's plate was almost empty as if he hadn't put anything on it.

"What are we doing today?" I asked Grandma Lyla. Then I put some food in my mouth.

"Well, I would like to go to Wal-Mart so I can cook dinner today," she said cleaning her plate and then putting it in the dishwasher. I nodded my head as I chewed. Grandma Lyla left to go somewhere in the house. I looked at Cole.

"What?" he asked.

"Nothing," I said back. He kept eating. Then I looked at him again. He put down his fork.

"Seriously, what?" he asked again.

"Can't you hear me? Nothing!" I said to him a little annoyed.

"Then why are you looking at me?"

"Can't I?"

"No, it's weird."

I rolled my eyes. Then Grandma Lyla came back.

"Guys, look at this," she said handing me a picture of a baby. He or she had a full head of hair.

"Who's this?" I asked.

"Look at it," Grandma Lyla said with a smile on her face.

"Dad?" I guessed. She shook her head no.

"Cutie-Colie, look at this picture," she said. Cole turned around. He put his plate in the sink and took the picture. He looked at it closer.

"I don't know...Alyssa?" He guessed. Grandma Lyla laughed.

"You think you look like your sister?" Grandma Lyla asked.

Cole's mouth fell open.

"This is me?" he asked. Grandma Lyla nodded her head. I didn't believe it myself.

"Can I see it?" I asked. Cole gave me his baby picture. I looked at it.

He had soft brown hair on top of his head. His green eyes had a ring of brown around the pupil and I thought they were so pretty compared to mine which were just flat out green. He had a little nose. It was so small, but big enough to touch and honk it. His freckles were spread from his nose to his cheeks. I looked up at him and still saw the same freckles. They were just a little more noticeable now.

"Yeah, that's him," I said giving him his picture.

"I was adorable!" he smiled.

"You aren't now," I said shaking my head like I was disappointed. He glared.

"Do you have a picture of me?" I asked.

"Of course! There are a lot of pictures of you in the living room," Grandma Lyla said. I smiled.

I ran to the living room. I saw a picture of me (I think) laying on my belly and my tiny little feet were in the air. I thought it was a blanket or something, but it looked like a white cloud covering my little tushy. My dark brown baby hair was curly instead of straight like Cole's hair. I looked at the left side of the picture.

I was four years old, sitting down. I had on a red summer dress with flowers on it. My curly hair came down to my neck. I had a big smile on my face. I looked down at the picture and saw I was holding a baby. The baby was peacefully sleeping. His head was small as I held it. Cole might've looked like a small baby but he was eight and a half pounds. He was heavy. So I took that picture and then looked for another one.

I found a picture of mommy holding him in her arms. This time, he was awake and smiling. He didn't have any clothes on except his diaper. I got that one too.

"Who do you think these are?" I asked him when I came back into the kitchen. He looked at them.

"This one is you and me obviously," he said and then took in a deep breath. "This baby Mom is holding is me," he smiled.

"So I guess you know who you are now, huh?" I said taking the pictures.

"I always knew myself!" he almost screamed. Oh my gosh! Second graders are sometimes stupid. Especially when you have one as a little brother.

"So can you guys go get dressed so we can go to Wal-Mart?" Grandma Lyla more likely said than asked. Cole and I smiled as if to say yes. I put the pictures back in the living room and then went upstairs.

Changes

I searched through my closet. I saw tights in there. I got them. Then I had to look for a shirt. I found a plaid shirt. It was basically pink with every other color like every other plaid shirt had. I put it on.

After getting dressed I brushed my hair. Usually, I would wear a ponytail, but I decided to leave it out today.

I came back down and found Grandma Lyla and Cole waiting for me.

"Finally, you're here. Girls are so slow," he said getting up.

"Boys are much slower. Just wait until they're in high school when they care about their hair," Grandma Lyla explained. I gave Cole a teasing smile. He frowned like the little baby that he obviously was.

I got in Grandma Lyla's old truck and sat in the front seat. Since Cole was only seven, he wouldn't be able to sit in the front seat until his eighth birthday. That was our family rule. It happened to me when I turned eight. But, when he can sit in the front seat we'll have to call shot gun. Yay! I'm pretty good with that. I always won with me and Kat. Right, I'm trying hard not to think about my friend, Kat.

As we rode to Wal-Mart, I looked around at the houses. The Christmas lights weren't on but I could tell they had them. I also saw Christmas wreaths around the doors. Oh, yeah! Christmas was almost here!

When Mom was alive we would cook Christmas dinner and then our whole family would come over. I loved those days. But since, Mom's been gone, we order Christmas dinner. Daddy never felt like cooking all that food so that began to be our new tradition.

About ten minutes later we finally reached Wal-Mart. We got out the truck and went inside. I liked shopping with Grandma Lyla so I was all in, a hundred percent on going shopping at Wal-Mart.

Cole ran to get the shopping cart when we were inside. He was in charge of the shopping cart. I was in charge of the list and the things we needed to get.

"Ready?" Grandma Lyla asked us.

"Oh yes!" Cole and I both said.

>>>>>

"Is that it?" Grandma Lyla asked. I looked at the list.

"Yeah. That's it," I said.

"Then let's go to the cashier," Grandma Lyla said while pushing the cart.

"I am tired," Cole said. I looked at him confused

"How in the world are you tired when it's only 11:45 in the morning?" I asked my hands on my hips.

"I don't know," he said shrugging his shoulders and jumping up and down. Once again, I rolled my eyes. We left Wal-Mart and went back to Grandma Lyla's house.

Right before we went inside her house, an older man called Grandma Lyla's name.

"Lyla!" he screamed. Grandma Lyla turned around.

"Oh, hello Robert," she said.

"Hey, how are you?" Robert said once he caught his breath. Grandma Lyla smiled.

"Good. Everything's great," she said. Then they just looked at each other. I looked at Cole.

"Do something," I whispered.

"No," he said back. Ugh!

"Ahem!" I cleared my throat to stop this awkward moment.

"Right!" Grandma Lyla perked up like nothing happened, "These are my grandchildren I told you about." I smiled and so did Cole.

"This is Alyssa my oldest and Cole my youngest," she continued.

"Hi, how are you?" I said nicely.

"Good, thank you. Now you guys should be thankful you have a grandmother like Lyla," Robert said taking my hand.

"Oh trust me, I am," I said.

"She is the best," Cole stepped in. Grandma Lyla blushed.

"So um Lyla?" Robert called her name again. "Can we talk privately?"

She looked at us. "Go inside guys. I'll bring the grocery bags in," Grandma Lyla said softly. Okay, whoa! Are Grandma Lyla and Robert gonna...no...right? Oh gosh!

I awkwardly smiled and went inside. Cole walked right behind me like a shadow.

"Do you think Grandma Lyla and Robert are gonna...I don't know...date?" I asked him.

"Pfft! No, they're old!" Cole said. We looked at each other.

"*YEAH*!" he and I said and then ran to the window.

We saw Grandma Lyla smiling and even laughing. Then she nodded her head yes at something.

"Shoot! I can't hear," I said.

"They might be talkin' 'bout the good old days," Cole said making a Texas accent. I laughed. Then we heard the door open. I jumped and so did Cole.

"What are you guys doing?" Grandma Lyla asked smiling. She had the grocery bags in her hand.

"We were looking at the birds outside," Cole lied.

I don't like lying so I went ahead and told the truth. "We were actually watching you," I said helping her. Cole's face turned red from lying. That embarrassed him. Grandma Lyla rolled her eyes.

"Robert is just a friend," she reassured us.

"Okay," Cole and I sang pretending to believe her. She smiled.

"Wanna cook dinner?" Grandma Lyla asked when we're in the kitchen.

"Yeah sure even though it's um only 12 o'clock," I said.

"Would you rather do it at 3 o'clock when you could be doing something else or um you know... now?" she asked.

"Now!"

"Good idea."

>>>>

"We're finally done!" Cole said falling onto the floor. Since he fell on the rug, he didn't get hurt. Should I be happy about that?

"Cole it's only 3 o'clock, the time we would've started," Grandma Lyla said.

"I don't care! I'm just happy that we're done!" he said like he was out of breath.

"You're just a big faker," I said to him. He made a pouty face at me and then said, "Does this look like a big faker to you?"

"Well now that you mention it... oh yes it still does," I said like I'm not phased, cause I'm not.

"Well you guys go do what you want and dinner is-**RING! RING!**" The house phone interrupted Grandma Lyla. She went over and answered it.

"Hello?" she asked. The only thing I heard was a squeaky voice.

"Oh hello, Joe. Yes, we're fine, thank you for checking on us," Grandma Lyla said. When I heard the name "Joe" I knew it was Daddy.

"Of course. Here he is," she said again and then gave the phone to Cole.

"Hi, Dad," Cole said and left the room. He always leaves the room like it's an important business call. Sometimes I wondered why I have the world's weirdest brother.

Then after a short while, he came back giving me the phone. Wow! That must be the world's shortest "business call."

"Did you have fun cooking?" Daddy asked when I put the phone to my ear.

"Yeah, I did. It was Cole who acted like it was a horror movie," I said Cole frowned. I smile. Daddy laughed.

"Cole just likes to eat," Daddy confirmed.

"Yeah, maybe too much," I said making a face at Cole.

"Well Honey, I got to go. Have fun with the rest of your day and I'll see you tomorrow," Daddy concluded the conversation.

"Okay. Bye, love you."

"Love you too," Daddy finished and then hung up. I put the phone away.

"What did you say I do too much?" Cole asked.

"Talk too much," I said adding to my list of "Things Cole Does Too Much." He frowned.

"And frowning," I added. He stomped away. Now I felt a little guilty.

But you can't let your guard down with Cole because he'll find a way to make you upset or annoyed. Trust me, it took me a couple of years to realize that.

I went upstairs. Mom's journal was peacefully laying on the nightstand. I picked it up to read. I was on page three now.

Dea-r Journal,

So today Riley asked me on the bus what would I name my daughter if I had one when I grew up. At first I told her I didn't know but I thought about what she said for the rest of the day. Finally, I got my answer... Alyssa. If I had a girl I would name her Alyssa. Hmm, good name, right? I like that name. But maybe when I'm older I would change it. Maybe. So, I gotta go. Bye.

-Kara

A big smile formed on my face. When she was younger she thought about naming me Alyssa...and she did! I am honored...so...so honored. I seriously didn't know what to say.

Since I had the rest of the day to myself, I took a nap. Now I was tired. Cooking could actually weigh you down. I laid my head down on my pillow and then I was knocked out.

»»»»

I got up from my nap and looked at the time. My heart shaped alarm clock said it was 5:26. My stomach growled. Time for dinner I guess.

I went downstairs and heard Grandma Lyla talking to someone. I looked closer and saw it was Robert. They must be "some kinda friends". Grandma Lyla saw me and smiled.

"How was your nap?" she asked. I smiled. She had probably checked on me while I was asleep.

"Good," I said. "Can I have dinner please?" I asked.

"Yeah. Let me call Cole to come eat too," Grandma Lyla said. I smiled.

"Hi Robert," I said not to be rude.

"Hello Alyssa," Robert said smiling. I sat down at the dining table. Cole came down looking tired. He plopped down next to me. Grandma Lyla fixed our plate.

"Thank you," I said when she gave me mine.

"Thank you," Cole said. We started to eat.

~3~

The next day came really quickly. Yesterday was fun though. We played Heads-Up with Robert and Grandma Lyla after eating. Heads-Up is pretty much like charades, except you have a card on your head. Anyway, Cole was on Robert's team, and I was with Grandma Lyla. Cole and Robert won but I personally think Grandma Lyla and I were awesome, and we had fun.

Now I'm in my room packing. Daddy was gonna pick us up in less than fifteen minutes. Yes, on Friday we came in the afternoon, but today is Sunday, and Cole and I had school tomorrow, so we had to leave early. If we didn't have school tomorrow we would either go home later or not go home at all.

"Knock, knock," Grandma Lyla said leaning on my door. I smiled.

"Hi," I said. She smiled too. Then her face became sad.

"What's wrong?" I asked She sat down on my bed.

"I wish your mother was here," she said.

Then my face turned sad too. I went over and gave her a hug. "Me too," I said under my breath. Grandma Lyla cried and so did I.

"So Allie can you..." Cole's voice trailed off when he saw me and Grandma Lyla hugging and crying. Grandma Lyla wiped her eyes and so did I.

"Are you guys okay?" Cole asked coming closer.

"Yeah, leave us alone," I said. Cole took a deep breath.

"Okay, but you suck at lying," he smiled.

"Come here, Cutie-Colie," Grandma Lyla said with her arms wide open. Cole gave her a hug. While they were hugging, I went over and got Mom's journal. I took it and put it in my suitcase. Then the doorbell rang.

I ran downstairs ready to see Daddy. I didn't open the door because you know the whole "don't open the door unless a grown-up is there" kind of rule. If you don't...well I have to follow that rule. Grandma Lyla came down all refreshed, like she had not shed a single tear. Then she opened the door.

Daddy was standing at the door texting. Then he saw us. I smiled. But come on! Daddy has been texting a lot lately. I wondered why. Maybe they were emails from other parents but I don't really think they email you that often unless your kid is like...you know...a monster. I'm now suspicious.

"Ready to come home?" Daddy asked.

"Of course," I said and then looked at Grandma Lyla. "Thank you for everything," I said smiling. She smiled too.

"Bye Grandma Lyla!" Cole said getting in the car. I waved goodbye to her and put my stuff in the car too. Then Daddy started talking to Grandma Lyla. I was already in the car as I watched them.

Grandma Lyla's face seemed serious and then it softened. She then gave Daddy a big smile and a hug. She also patted his back. Hmm, I wondered what he told her? Daddy's face was also lit up and happy. Oh, wow! Whatever he told her, he must be beyond happy! Seriously, what did he tell her?

I watched Daddy get in the car and start it. He was still smiling.

"You guys had fun, didn't you? Grandma Lyla told me that you guys were good so I'll take you out to dinner later," Daddy said. Cole and I smiled. I loved going out to dinner. It was always fun.

"Daddy, did you know that Mom had a journal?" I asked when were at the traffic light.

"Yeah, she had multiple. Did Grandma Lyla give you one of hers?" he asked drumming on the steering wheel.

"Yeah."

"Which one?"

"The one where she's in middle school."

Daddy stopped talking. His face turned red for some reason. I had only ever seen this happen to him when he was really mad at me.

"Look at Dad," I whispered to Cole. He did and then his mouth turned into a big O.

"What did you say to him...you broke him?!" Cole asked glaring at me.

"Nothing, except that Mom had a journal when she was in middle school," I explained.

"Dad? Daddy...are you okay?" I asked. He jumped.

"Yeah, yeah. I'm fine," he said, his face returning back to its normal color. I wasn't convinced.

"You know your face turned red, right?" I said making sure he was aware.

"Oh, it did...oh okay," Daddy said and then stepped on the gas. I wanted to ask why it had turned red but... I just kept quiet.

» » »

When we got home, and we unloaded the car. Everything was normal now. Tomorrow was school; we wouldn't see Grandma until Christmas which was in two whole days. So again everything was a-okay.

I'm in my room right now reading a book. No, it's not Mom's journal, but it's my favorite author, Majae Locke. She writes really awesome books. The best thing, though, was that she was only like thirteen years old.

"Hey, Allie?" Daddy said coming in with Cole beside him. His face looked serious. I put down my book.

"Yeah?" I said a little concerned. He sat down. Then he got up again.

"Let's go down and sit in the family room," he said. I followed him. Okay, I'm now a little scared. What happened? Had Grandma Lyla fallen down the stairs? Had he lost his job? What was it?! What was it!?

I sat down and Cole sat next to me. His little tiny face actually serious and concerned for once. That meant whatever Dad was about to spill out was dead on serious. I took a deep breath in and then let it out. Okay, I'm ready...give it to me. I looked at Dad. His beautiful chocolaty brown eyes seemed like they could see through my soul.

"So guys," he began, "after your mother died, I thought I would never really love anyone again," he said and then took a deep breath. "But that has changed," he said, as he let it out.

"I have. About a year ago, I met a woman," he said and then smiled.

I gasped. This was my worst nightmare. I *knew* someday... any day, he would meet someone again and fall in love. I knew he was gonna let Mom go and he would forget about her. At the back of my eyes tears were stinging and building up to break free. No-no-no!

"Her name is Olivia. She's a beautiful woman and you guys will love her," he said his cheeks smiling all the way up to his eyes. I looked at Cole. He was shocked too, but not like I was. I don't know if he was looking forward to Daddy meeting a new woman or not, but I knew that I wasn't.

"Do you have a picture of her?" I asked.

"That's the other thing. I'm not gonna show a picture of her to you guys," he said. I'm confused now.

"What are you gonna do then?" I asked. He smiled.

"You're gonna meet her...today!" He said. My mouth turned into an O. First, he was dating a woman and it had been going on for a year now. Second, I'm not allowed to see her picture but I'm gonna meet her...today? Whoa! Just...whoa.

"That's it?" Cole asked.

"No," Daddy said looking down and rubbing his hands on his thighs. "I'm gonna...I'm gonna marry her," he finished. Now Cole's eyes jumped out his face. I fainted.

»»»

"Alyssa?" called a voice.

"Hey, you okay?" Daddy asked.

"Is it true?" I asked him.

"I knew you were gonna have a hard time with this," he said.

"Why?" I asked.

"I love her Alyssa...and you will too," he said. I felt like laughing in his face. What would he know about who'll I'll love? What does he know? I sat up. And I then started asking more questions.

"Does she have children?"

"Yes."

"How many?"

"Two. Beauti and Bella."

"Does she know about me and Cole?"

"Of course," he frowned. Then I gave him the number one question.

"Does she know about Mom?" I asked. He squinted.

"Why wouldn't she?" he answered.

"So she does. Okay," I said and then got up. I started to go upstairs.

"Get dressed, Alyssa. We'll be meeting them at dinner," he said.

"I wish we weren't," I said under my breath.

I felt like crying. But I thought about it and put it all together. My dad was marrying a woman named Olivia, that he had been dating for a year and hadn't told us until now. And then this "Olivia" has two children Beauti and Bella. Now pause, "What kind of name is Beauti...what?" Anyway, Cole, Daddy, and I were all gonna go out for dinner, but apparently, Olivia was gonna join us so we could meet her. Oh gosh. I wonder if her children were coming too. This was a lot to process. No wonder I had passed out.

"Can you believe it? We're gonna have a new mother," Cole said as he came into my room smiling. I frowned. How could he?

"No, I don't believe it and I don't wanna," I said crossing my arms.

"Why are you so upset?" he asked.

"This woman could be a monster! Our lives could be like Cinderella...without a happy ending by the way," I said.

"You seriously think Olivia is gonna be a monster?" he asked actually waiting for my answer instead of blabbing on.

I raised an eyebrow at him.

"You're cold as ice. You won't even give the woman a chance," Cole said and then left. I started to cry. He didn't understand. Obviously, he didn'tknow how it was to lose someone you truly loved. He was only two when she died.

»»»

By the time Dad came into my room, I was already dressed. He gave me a small smile. I was about to put my hair in a ponytail when he stopped me.

"Do you really wanna wear your hair up in a ponytail while wearing a beautiful dress? Leave it down. You look great," he smiled. I left it down but I wouldn't look at him. He came over and put a strand of hair behind my ear.

"You'll love her...Seriously," he said his hands on my shoulder. I still wouldn't look up. His soft hands gently pushed up my chin to look at him.

"I love you," he said. Now I had to say something.

"Love you too," I said. Even though I was mad at him I meant it. He smiled and gave me a hug messing up my hair. I couldn't help but smile too. When he was done I went into the bathroom to brush my hair. My hair did look nice down with my pretty white dress.

I went downstairs and saw Cole in a tuxedo looking like Daddy but mini. It was cute. You could see the gel on his dark brown hair a little bit.

"Ready?" Daddy asked.

"Do I have a choice?" I said.

"Not really," he said and then opened the front door. I took in a deep breath and let it out. We got in the car and left.

We reached the restaurant. When I got out of the car I saw that the place was full already. I headed toward the door but Daddy stopped me. He pointed to a beautiful table with a nice looking candle. There were six chairs around the round table. Hmm, we're gonna be outside huh? I went ahead and sat down. Cole again sat next to me.

"Alyssa," Daddy called my name, "be very kind. Don't embarrass me, okay?" he warned.

"Okay," I said.

As we waited I saw a lot of people coming in and going out. I didn't know which one was Olivia, Bella or Beauti, so I just waited. We waited about five minutes when we saw a taxi cab.

A woman in a tight red dress with blonde hair stepped out. She had on red boots that came up to her knees. Coming out behind her was a girl about age thirteen who also had blonde hair but it was lighter and in a ponytail. I glared at Daddy. He told me I should wear my hair down, but that girl could wear a ponytail? So unfair. Next was a young girl about age six coming out. Again, she had blonde hair. What was this a Blondie-Fest?

They started to walk towards us. I gasped and my heart started to beat...fast. Them? The Blondie-Family? Ugh! I looked at Daddy who was just staring while smiling at the woman in the red dress. I guessed that was Olivia. He got up and so did Cole and I.

"I'm so happy to see you, Olivia," Daddy said giving her a hug. She smiled.

"Me too, Joey," Olivia said. Joey? Is that what she's gonna call my dad? This was gonna be a long night. Oh, by the way, his real name is Joseph. When they stopped hugging she looked at Cole.

"Cole right?" she asked. Cole nodded his head yes. She knelt down and said "I've heard so many stories about you. You have such an attractive face for a seven-year-old," she said. Cole said thank you and gave her a hug. She kissed the top of his head...just like I remember Mom doing when we left to go to Grandma Lyla's the night of the accident. Then she came to me.

Face to face I looked at her. She looked nothing like my mother but she was a pretty woman with bright blue eyes like the sky. Her lips were dark pink like Barbie's closet. She had rosy pale skin instead of my tan skin. What I'm saying is that she's much lighter. But skin color does not matter to me.

"You're Alyssa," she said smiling while saying my name. "What a pretty name. Who named you?"

"My mother," I said taking in all the details of her face.

"I'm sorry about your mother Alyssa. I really am, so I will do the best I can to be the perfect mother for you," she said.

"You mean stepmother," I corrected her. She looked at Daddy with a small smile. He mouthed to her, "I told you so."

"Yes. Stepmother. Meet my daughters. Please," she said moving out of the way. Then I saw the girls.

"This is Beauti," she said pointing to the one who looked like a thirteen-year-old. Beauti, with an obviously fake smile, waved at me. I waved back. She was like two inches taller than me. Her ponytail lay down on her chest.

"And then my youngest, Bella," she said. Bella was standing, there a big smile on her face. She came and gave me a hug. Oh, no, another Cole, except girl version. Now I put a fake smile on my face and gently hugged her back.

"Ever since I heard about you, I wanted to meet you. Now I'll have two sisters," she said in a very jolly tone. I smiled.

"Well, I just heard about you today and really wasn't looking forward to this," I wanted to say but didn't. So I just smiled.

Changes

"Are you guys hungry because I heard this place has amazing food," Dad said sitting back down. Beauti sat on the other side of me. I looked at her. She was texting under the table but that's not what I was looking at. I was looking at her face. Now I know why she was named Beauti. The girl was gorgeous for crying out loud! I saw her mom look at her.

"Stop and talk," she mouthed. Since I'm good at reading lips, I kinda knew what she said to Beauti. Beauti moaned a little, but not loud enough that her mom could hear, but I could. She put away her phone and looked at me.

"So...like how old are you?" She asked me, not really caring but just forced to make conversation.

"Eleven," I said getting my hair out of my face. She raised her eyebrows like she wasn't phased or anything. I looked at her. "You?" I asked.

"Thirteen," she said and then grabbed her phone again. I knew it! So, now I had no one to talk to. I looked over at Cole and found him babbling away with Bella. It's like he got a twin. I looked down. This seriously was like the **worst** dining out experience ever!

"So Alyssa, what do you like to do?" Olivia asked as she put food in her mouth. I raised my head to find her eyes.

"I like to do a lot of different stuff," I said hopefully to stop her from going on. Again she looked at me.

"Allie usually likes to read," Dad stepped in. I smiled awkwardly.

"Beauti here, loved to read until she got her phone and then she would never stop texting," Olivia said and then raised her voice at the "stop texting" part. Beauti looked up and found everyone looking at her.

"I like to talk," she added.

"Yeah, but only to your weird friends," Bella said. Beauti growled at her. Bella looked at her and smiled. Rolling her eyes, Beauti looked at her mom. Olivia shook her head. Beauti slumped in her seat.

"So...I see your hair is very long," Beauti said. Awkwardly I smiled again.

Combing it out with my hand I said to her, "I'll ask Daddy to take me to get it cut." Her eyes became big.

"No, you shouldn't. You could be like Rapunzel with brown hair," she said smiling for real.

"Thanks. Your hair is long too," I said. She raised an eyebrow.

"No, it's not," she said and then took it out of its ponytail. Her hair streamed down to her chest. Blonde hair is so pretty.

"To me, you look like Princess Aurora," I said.

"I hate her," she said. Oops! Wrong thing to say.

"Okay, not Aurora but maybe Cinderella?" I asked.

"Stop with the princess names!" she blew up at me. I gasped. This is why I never bring down my guards. Olivia saw we weren't talking anymore and she didn't push us by the look on our faces. Good! Already I can tell I'm not liking this so far. Nothing is a-okay and it'll never be from now on!

»»»

We went inside our house without Olivia, Beauti, or Bella. I just met them and already I needed a break from them. I took off my jacket and started upstairs. I changed into my pajamas.

I was brushing my hair when Cole came in my room. He looked so happy. Well, good for him. He'd had a good time. But I had the worst dining out experience ever! Seriously, like someone was just trying to make more conversation after you gave them a real smile that's not fake, but then you go and blow up at them! Who does that...oh right, Beauti!

"Bella is so fun. She gets me so much. And then Olivia is so nice and sweet! After everything Bella told me about Beauti I realized you and her are so much alike," Cole said.

I frowned, confused. "Beauti and I are nothing alike so don't you dare say that," I scolded him.

He raised an eyebrow confused. Then smiled like he understood. "Right, you're nothing alike. She's more Beautiful!" Cole had cracked a stupid joke. He laughed and I pretended to laugh too.

"Yeah, yeah and Bella is smarter than you because when she thinks, she actually rings a bell...but you don't even think... because you don't have a brain," I said.

He stopped laughing and looked at me. "That's not funny. I'm not saying that because you used her against me but because you just suck at coming up with jokes," he said and then left. I frowned. For once I agreed with him. I sighed. Laying my head down I thought about today. Then I changed my mind. "No, never mind," I said to myself.

The next day my alarm clock made the hair on my body stand up and my eardrums ache as it woke me up. I poked the air not realizing that my hand wasn't even near the alarm clock. I dragged my head up like it was impossible for me to keep it up. I touched the 'dismiss' button and the alarm clock stopped blaring. As soon as I touched it my head dropped back down.

I promise you that I am seriously allergic to Mondays. I hate them so much. And yes, the fact that I went to dinner yesterday with the Blondie-Fest people made today even worse. When I thought maybe I could sleep for five more minutes, Daddy's voice boomed from downstairs.

"Come on Alyssa! No more five minutes. That was an elementary school excuse," he said. Sometimes I wondered if that man could read my mind without even looking at me. I got up and did my morning routine.

On my way downstairs, I couldn't help but look into Cole's room. He was in his bed playing a video game. I raised an eyebrow.

"You have three more minutes of your five minutes thingy. I would take all I've got," I said.

"Well, that's you. I don't do the 'five minutes thingy'," he said his fingers poking the air making air quotes.

"All I'm saying is that you should use it while you can. When you get to middle school you're gonna beg for the 'five minutes thingy'," I said copying his air quote.

"All I'm saying is...no I won't," he said looking at me with boredom in his eyes. Ugh! He is so...ugh! I'm a big sister, right? Yeah, so I try to give my younger and insanely annoying brother advice, but he just shakes it off like Taylor Swift. I went downstairs. When he gets to middle school and begs for the 'five minutes thingy' I will make fun of him so much he'll cry to make me stop.

"Come on! I gotta get to my classroom. Where's Cole? His five minutes are up," Daddy said in a rush. "Cole!" he screamed and then growled. Then his face lit up. "I'll be right back," he said to me. I grabbed a bowl and a cereal box. I poured my milk in my bowl and started to eat.

"Oh great. Thank you so much. So sorry I had called out of the blue," I heard Daddy say when he came back. I forced myself to turn around and saw him putting away his phone. He came and touched my shoulder. I kept eating.

"I called Olivia to see if she could give you a ride to school," he said.

My eyes bolted out of my head and I almost choked on my colorful delicious Froot Loop Cereal. Swallowing really hard I managed to ask, "What about Cole?"

"Cole still goes to elementary school so he's with me," Daddy said and then screamed Cole's name one more time. Cole came downstairs.

"Come on, Olivia will be here in less than five minutes to pick up Allie," Daddy said. Cole looked at me.

"You're going with Olivia? You're lucky!" he said.

"Am I? Am I really?" I wanted to say so badly but bit my lips to keep them from parting.

Then in a blink of an eye, a white minivan showed up at our driveway. I saw Olivia's blonde hair through the car. She got out and started walking. Daddy, Cole and I walked out. Daddy locked the door. I swung my book bag over my shoulders and the other strap half sagged as I walked.

"Livvy, Baby, thank you again. So I already sent you the address to her school and she knows where to go," Daddy said kissing Olivia's left cheek. I wondered if they have ever kissed on the lips...it's a fifty-fifty chance that they have. Olivia looked at me.

"I am delighted to drive her to school. It let's me know how it'll feel once she becomes my daughter," Olivia said her crystal clear teeth sparkling. I could've said step-daughter, but she had beaten me to it.

"So... um... Cole and I gotta roll... So bye," Daddy said. I gave him a hug. Cole waved at Olivia and at me. We were still getting in the car when they vanished out of sight.

I got in Olivia's minivan. It had the new car smell. I wanted to ask if she had just bought this car, but I wasn't trying to make conversation. Because I have learned that one thing leads to another and I didn't want to head down any road with Olivia. She hesitated to put on the radio.

"What radio station do you listen to?" she asked me.

"Ninety-four point five, PST," I said. Olivia's face lit up as she smiled.

"Beauti loves this station. Doesn't it play music by Nicki Minaj, Selena Gomez and what's her name? Ahh, I can't remember! I believe it starts with a D," she said. I knew who she was talking about.

"Demi Lovato," I said like it was my name.

"Yes, her! Bella likes her but Beauti likes Nicki Minaj. I don't know why and then they're always fighting over who's better. Personally, I think both singers are great," Olivia babbled. I kept quiet.

"Who do you like?" she asked.

"I don't have a favorite. I like them all minus one," I said.

"Who's the minus one?" she asked.

"Katy Perry. I like some of her songs but not her. I really don't like her," I said.

"Oh," Olivia breathed out. She didn't try to say anything else. We spent the rest of the car ride quiet. Olivia hummed some of the songs.

"It's a love robbery," I sang under my breath. I loved this song. It's Love Robbery by Kalin and Myles. Olivia laughed. I looked at her.

"You have been singing for the last two minutes," she said. My face turned fire red. Ugh! Why didn't she leave me alone? I saw that we were almost at school and I almost cried from happiness.

"Turn right here," I said at the corner. Then we pulled into my school. I got out the car and started walking towards school. Then I remembered something. Whenever you're in the car line, whoever brought you to school or took you home had to sign you in.

I told Olivia the whole situation and she smiled. She got out the car and walked inside my school. I sat down on the seat in the office. The principal came out and looked at Olivia.

"Who are you?" Mr. Brown asked.

"I am Olivia Holden. Uh, Joseph Halse's fiancée," Olivia said. My principal broke into a smile.

"Right. Mr. Halse has told me he is now engaged," Mr. Brown said and then looked at me. "You are happy aren't you now?" I smiled just to be nice. Olivia finished signing me in and then left. She waved bye, and I waved back as I put a fake smile on my face.

I was walking down the hallway when Kat caught up to me.

"Hey," she said.

"Hi," I said back just a little confused. Why was she talking to me after that fight we had last week?

"Sorry about last week, ok? It just seems like we don't see eye to eye anymore, right?" she said.

"Yeah, me too. I'm sorry. Last week was a weird week for me," I said. She looked at me and then one of her cheerleader friends screamed her name.

"Bye gotta go!" she said in a hurry as she ran back down the hallways. I told her bye. I felt like I had no friends anymore. Like, Kat was the only friend I had and cared about. Now she and I didn't even agree on one sentence anymore so of course we barely talked anymore. It was just me, myself and I.

I walked into math class. Then I remembered that I forgot my math homework. No! Now I was gonna have to do it at lunch. Life is great isn't it? I sat in my seat and realized that my world was just falling apart! I don't know if I can even keep up with it. I sighed unhappily.

~4~

I sadly walk to lunch. I didn't feel good today. My stomach was stuck in a knot and my head was hurting. But, I could go through the rest of day. I stood in line to get my lunch and as soon as I got it, I walked to a table. No one was sitting there so it was just me. I stared down at my math homework and groaned. But I sucked it up and looked at number one.

I went to put my chicken nugget in my mouth and as I swallowed it, the whole thing came back up again. I looked at the floor covered in my throw up. Everyone at the other tables held their noses, screamed "eeewww" and just kept staring at me. A teacher came up to me and angrily ordered me to go to the nurse.

The nurse said that I had a fever and she was calling Daddy. But it was only 12:45. Daddy was still working. Hopefully, he would come and not Olivia. I told her Daddy's number and she called him. He said that he wss coming. I smiled in relief that it was him. This day was just awful. In fact, my whole life has been horrible since Mom died.

"Are you ok? I am pretty sure that the food didn't do this today," Daddy asked looking straight ahead and not at me in the car. I wasn't sure what to say. I didn't know what to say or think!

"I think you need to start talking to me Alyssa," Daddy said when he stopped the car as the traffic light turned red. He looked at me. I looked at him.

"I'm fine. Thanks," I said with a fake smile. He sighed not convinced.

"I'm here for you..." he said and then put his hand over mine. This is it! I have to tell him I don't want him and Olivia together. I don't want Beauti or Bella to become my step sisters. I opened my mouth to say something but Daddy's phone buzzed and jumped in his coat. He answered.

"Yeah, she's fine...yes, of course. It's just a little fever," he said to this person. By how it was going, I guessed Olivia. He hung up saying, "I love you" to whoever he was talking to so I immediately knew it was Olivia. Daddy looked at me and said,

Changes

"Were you about to say something before?" I told him no, even though that was when I could've told him.

I got home and just felt like I didn't want to be here. I got inside and started to go upstairs, but Daddy stopped me.

"You're going to stay in bed because of that small fever," he said. I had forgotten about that. I didn't argue. I listened as he told me what to do. We then went upstairs and, I got my temperature taken again. It was better than what it was in school, but Daddy told me to go lay in the bed for a little while.

I am now upstairs watching TV, but my eyes are slowly getting tired and it's almost impossible for me to keep my head up. I slowly sank into my pillow and my eyes start to shut down and so does my body.

»»»

I woke up to see Cole right in front of me. I groaned telling him to go away. Why is he here anyway?

"Dad wanted me to see if you're awake," he explained.

"I'm awake okay, now go away," I shouted at him.

"Geez, okay. Just stay in bed until Dad comes," he said.

I groaned again. That nap was okay. I looked at the time and saw that it was 3:00 PM. I could've kept sleeping but no, I had to be woken up. Then, Daddy came in, followed by Olivia. Oh my Lord, will she just **LEAVE** us alone?!

"Hey, how are you feeling?" Daddy asked concern in his eyes.

"Good."

"Good," he said and then looked at Olivia, "We are going to cook Christmas dinner this year." My eyes opened wide as a smile rose on my face. Yay! Then I frowned.

"Is Olivia going to cook with us?" I tried to say without attitude, but let me just tell you, it felt impossible not to.

"Yes and so is Beauti and Bella," he said. My stomach didn't feel good again.

"Are they here?"

"Yes Alyssa, they are. And Beauti will be a lot nicer to you," Olivia jumped in. Yes, Beauti and I had small issues, but, how did Olivia know that we had problems? Had she eavesdropping on us the other day? I didn't know, but it sounded like it.

"Can I get out of bed now?" I asked wiggling under the covers.

"Let me get your temperature," Olivia said.

"Oh no! No, no, no! She will not. Please, Daddy don't let her," I silently screamed.

"Okay I'll be downstairs starting to make the food," he said as he interrupted my thoughts. Dang it!

Olivia walked out to get the thermometer. She put it in my mouth. I hoped my temperature was back to normal because I was so embarrassed. Thankfully, it was back to normal. I smiled and started to get out of the bed.

"Now Alyssa, please take it easy," Olivia said with a small smile on her face. I nodded my head yes and then I ran downstairs. I smelled my dad's famous lasagna and heard laughter. I saw Daddy talking to Beauti, Bella, and Cole. They all had smiles on their faces. I had missed something good.

"Oh hi, Alyssa!" Bella chirped happily at me. I said hi back and sat down on one of the chairs. Beauti glanced at me not sure what to say so she said, "Want to hear a joke?"

"Sure, I guess," I replied.

"So, there was a lion, a mouse, and a snake. The mouse said to the lion 'Will you eat me?' And the lion said 'No.' What did the snake say?" Beauti said pausing and looking at me.

"I dunno. What did he say?"

"The snake said to the mouse 'Don't listen to him, he's **LION**!' Get it?" she said. I laughed understanding it and so did Bella, Cole, and Daddy. That was corny but I got it and it was somewhat funny.

"Works all the time," Beauti said looking at her nails with a satisfied smile on her face.

Olivia came down holding something. I saw it in her hand...my mom's journal.

"Joey, did you know that Kara had a journal?" she asked again. Dad turned red.

"Uh, yeah. She um...she liked writing...a lot," he said, not looking at Olivia, but at the stove.

"Where'd you find that?" I asked.

"In your room," she said. I frowned. How dare she snoop around my room! Nothing in there was any of her business.

"Can I please have it back?" I asked. She came over and gave it to me. I "accidentally" snatched it out of her hand. Now I had to put my stuff in private places. Ugh, why?!

"Since you're still sick Sugar, I think you should um just stay low profile so your little germs won't get in the food," Olivia said to me. My mouth dropped into an O. What? I always helped cook Christmas dinner. I looked at Dad to help me but he didn't say anything. She's changing him!

I didn't say anything but went and sat on the couch. I turned on the TV and relaxed. This was so boring! Olivia was telling Beauti to stir the sauce for the spaghetti. And dad showed Cole how to cut the onions. And Bella was the one setting the flowers on the table. I was doing...nothing. I decided to go outside. I sat on the front porch.

I felt like I was forgotten. Like, like, no one wanted me. I wanted to get out of there and I wanted to leave! I wanted to leave Dad and his new family. Just then, Daddy came out and sat next to me. I looked at the time and actually realized I had been out here for almost an hour. Wow!

"We're going to set up the tree. You want to help?" he asked. I snickered.

"Are you sure? I mean, I don't want to get my germs on it. Oh, no, no. That would be bad wouldn't it?" I said with sarcasm.

"Stop it, Alyssa. I know you're upset, but what Olivia said was right. But since we're done with the food part you can now help," he said.

"Whatever," I mumbled. He shook his head.

"Join us when your sarcasm showcase is over," he said and then went back inside.

I am not going back inside. I am not joining them. They obviously don't want me. So, why in the world should I go back inside? The door opened again.

"Dad I heard you, but I'm not going back inside. I don't want to," I said.

"Well, will you at least care to tell me why?" Olivia's silky voice echoed a little throughout the neighborhood as she sat next to me. I looked at her.

"No."

"Look...Alyssa. I know you miss your mother. I understand," she started, "but you have to give me a chance. I don't even know why you hate me so much. I never did anything to you so...please talk to me," she begged. I took in a deep breath.

"I don't hate you," I said, "this is...all new to me. And I'm glad Dad found you. I can see he's happy with you. You're awesome it's just..." I stopped.

"Just what?"

"I loved my mother very much! And when she was gone I broke down. I felt like I died too. And now that Dad is gonna marry you, you're gonna be my mother. But what if something happens to you too? What will I do then?" I asked tears in my eyes.

"Oh Sweetie come here," she said her arms wide open. I went and gave her a hug. She stroked my hair lightly as she said, "Please don't worry about that. I am here, aren't I? And everyone will die one day. But not right now, so live your life to the fullest, okay?" I nodded yes. She kissed the top of my head.

"Now, can we please go decorate the tree?" she asked with a big smile on her face.

"Wait there's more," I said. "I don't think Beauti likes me."

"Oh, she does. Let me assure you. She just has to get used to it. And you should start talking to her okay?" she pressed.

"Okay."

"Now *PLEASE* let's go decorate a tree?" I laughed at her, and said, "Yes."

We went inside holding hands. A smile grew on Daddy's face. Bella came and grabbed my hand. She showed me where to put the ornaments.

"You okay?" Beauti asked when we were decorating the tree.

"Yeah, I'm...a lot better. I feel a lot better."

"Good," she said and then surprised me. She gave me a hug.

"Aww," Daddy said. He ran to go get the camera. He came back and took the picture. When we were all done, we took a family picture. And I...I felt happy.

»»»

"I'm staying in Alyssa's room right?" Beauti asked.

"Yes Beauti," Olivia said with tiredness in her voice. Beauti squealed in excitement and gave me a hug. I smiled.

So, since tomorrow's Christmas, Olivia decided to sleep over at our house. Bella, Beauti, Cole, and I got so excited. Ever since I had that talk with Olivia, Bella, Beauti and I all got along much better. It was like were best friends. But even better, they're now my sisters. Um, I meant soon to be step-sisters. I'm so excited! Tomorrow's Christmas!

"Night Bella...Alyssa...and last but not least...Beauti," Dad said kissing us on top of our heads. We all said at the same time, "Goodnight."

He left and then it was Olivia's turn.

"Mommy, I'm so glad we're spending Christmas here!" Bella said her squeaky voice the only sound in my room. Beauti and I looked at each other and smiled...real smiles.

"Yeah, me too," Beauti added.

"Me three!" I said at last. We all laughed. Olivia said goodnight to us and then turned out the light.

"Mommy no!" Bella squealed.

"Alyssa, do you have a night light?" Olivia asked. I nodded my head yes and got up. I looked in one of my drawers and I got one. I took it and turned it on.

"Thanks."

"You're welcome," I said as the door closed. I laid back down between Bella and Beauti.

"My gosh, I'm so excited!" Bella said, "I'm not going to fall a....(yawn) sleep," and then her eyes closed. I looked at Beauti for explanation.

"She does that every Christmas Eve," Beauti said. I giggled.

"So, Alyssa who's your best friend again?" Beauti asked. I stopped to look at her. Earlier today she asked who was my best friend. I told her right now I had none. I told her I used to have Kat and about everything that tore us apart.

"Katrina," I said.

"Don't worry about her. Besides you have me and Bella," she said. A smile grew on my face.

"You're right," I agreed with her.

"And since you're moving to our house, you'll go to a new school and everything, you'll have new friends too," she said.

"Yeah...wait what?" I said in shock.

"Oh I forgot to tell you," she started. She sat up, crisscrossed, apple sauced and continued telling me.

"The other day I heard Mom and Dad talking...your dad. And Mom thinks it's a better idea if you guys move in with us since our house is bigger and has more room for you guys. And your dad will be able to still go to his job, Cole can still go to the same elementary school, but you have to go to the Middle School I'm in. I'm in 8th grade," she clarified.

I looked at her shocked. I'm not going to Rexha Middle School anymore. Whoo Hoo! Yes! I went and gave Beauti a hug.

"Now I can start over! I can just be Alyssa Halse. Not The-Girl-Who-Lost-Her-Mother!" I gushed in happiness. Beauti frowned.

"They called you that?"

"Oh yeah and *MANY* more."

"People are evil!"

"Tell me about it," we both laugh and then I turned off the night light.

»»»

"Get up!" Bella shook me awake. Then she went to Beauti.

"People get up!" she quietly yelled. Beauti rubbed her eyes. I looked at her and could've bet that she was another person because she looked like a beast. Her hair was literally standing on top of her head. Mine looked...pretty decent!

"Come on, I want to go downstairs to see if Santa came!" Bella whined.

"Bella we have to brush our teeth first," Beauti said.

"Nooo," Bella whined even more.

"Hey! Mom said if she's sleeping, I'm in charge. So what I say goes," Beauti said dead serious, her piercing blue eyes looked very scary. Bella groaned and went into the bathroom to brush her teeth. I followed her and whispered in Beauti's ear.

"Is that true? You're in charge?"

"Yeah. I try not to boss her around, but Bella can get very whiny and can be insanely annoying."

"I feel you. I mean like, Cole is exactly the same,"

"Double trouble!"

"Mm hmm," we said in unison. Then we laughed. We were suddenly best friends now!

We all brushed our teeth and hair. Then we heard the door open. Olivia walked out wearing a long purple robe followed by Daddy who was wearing a long black robe.

"Good morning guys," they both said at the same time.

"Morning," Beauti said.

"Good morning," Bella said.

"Good morning," I smiled.

We looked at them like, "Can We Go Downstairs! Please?"

They both laughed and said, "Yeah."

We ran downstairs bumping into each other. I believe I almost fell down the stairs because Bella was like a MONSTER going down.

We saw Cole sitting in the living room. He looked up and gave us a goofy, tired, smile. He had those blackish purplish round rings around his eyes. He didn't look so good.

"I've been awake for...(counts his fingers) three hours, waiting for you guys!" he almost shrieked.

"So you've been awake since 6:00 AM?" Beauti asked. He slowly nodded his head yes.

"Sorry, but you've got problems," she sat down on one of the couches. I went over and sat next to her. Bella sat next to Cole.

"I got the camera, so let's start opening the presents," Daddy said rubbing his hands together with a big smile on his face. Olivia smiled too.

"Shell-Belle should go first. Let's start by youngest to oldest," Olivia said.

"Aww!" We all groaned but Bella. Well of course, not her. She's six! So next would be Cole, then me, and then Beauti. I knew she didn't like that.

Bella got cool new sneakers she had apparently been begging Olivia to get. They were so pretty. They were bright purple, had tints of other colors and looked like the galaxy. And then she got an American Girl Doll that had the same blonde hair and blue eyes as she did.

90

Cole got brand new video games that he could play with Daddy for the next couple of days before school started again. Then he got a skateboard that Daddy would teach him how to ride. Now it was my turn.

It was a red small box with Christmas trees on it. Okay? Well, it's nothing like Bella and Cole's big box. Different ideas were racing through my mind. Wondering what could be in here, I ripped it faster and faster. Then a picture of an iPhone, one of the latest models, caught my eye. I couldn't believe it. I blinked a few times making sure I was seeing right. I looked at it again and opened the box. A golden iPhone shined up at me. I took it out of the box and held it. I went over and gave Daddy a hug telling him thank you, over and over again.

"Oh no, it was not my idea," Daddy started as I looked at him, "but it was Olivia's idea. And she's going to tell you why she got it but she deserves all the thanks and much more," he finished. I looked at Olivia and smiled.

"Thank you so much," I said my arms around her neck. She laughed and told me, "You're welcome."

"What did you get?" Bella said coming over. And they all came forward. I showed them my new phone with a smile on my face. Bella gushed out a "Wow" as Cole shrugged his shoulders as if he was not impressed. But he's my brother and under those green tinted brown eyes, I knew he was impressed and maybe a little jealous.

"Don't worry Cole, I'll let you play with my phone," I said. He huffed as if he was not interested and I smiled. Beauti smiled and said, "Congratulations."

"Why did you get me a phone?" I asked.

"I'll explain that later, but right now, I would like to see Beauti open her gift," she said. Beauti smiled.

I watched her tear apart the wrapper the gift was in, her eyes hungry to see what she got.

It was an instrument. And by the shape of it... it was a violin. I raised my eyebrows in shock. Does Beauti even know how to play that? I mean, she had to or how else was she going to play it? But then, she could get lessons. Her face kept her smile. She said thank you to her mom and then played a little song on the violin. When she finished we all clapped. It was good. She was good. The sound was so flawless and beautiful that you couldn't resist listening...you just could not!

Then she opened another box. It was books. Like a lot of books. Her face lit up even more.

"I know you still like to read," her mom said. They looked at each other and you could see and feel a strong bond between them that would never be broken.

"I've always wanted to read this series. Since I was ten," she said.

"Yes, but you have to be thirteen to read that series. And last time I checked...someone is thirteen," Olivia smiled. Beauti gave her a LONG hug.

"Now!" Dad broke the silence making all of us jump, "Olivia, please tell them the news," he said.

"We are going to live together. In my house," she said.

"...That means Alyssa, Cole, and Dad are going to live with us?" Bella said. Olivia nodded yes. I wasn't mad because Beauti had already told me this and I didn't mind. I wanted to move. I wanted to start over.

Changes

But when I looked over to Cole, the idea didn't sit well with him. I could see it in his face. His excitement, just plunged down into the earth. He looked at me tears in his eyes.

"I'm going to the bathroom," he said leaving. Lie. That was a lie. I followed him without a word.

~5~

"Leave me alone," he said wiping away his tears. I was going to try to make him laugh but I didn't think it would work.

"You know I can't get away from you. We're siblings!" I said. I got nothing but a glare. See, I told you so!

"Cole it's not so bad to move. Besides, you're still going to go to the same elementary school," I said rubbing my hand on his shoulder.

"What?"

"Oh, you're still going to the same school. But I'm not. I'm going to a new middle school," I tried to explain as best as I could.

"How do you know? They didn't say that."

"Beauti overheard Daddy and Olivia talking and she told me last night."

"Oh, okay," he said and then left. I nodded my head. He didn't even say thank you for the information, I just provided him. As much as I loved him he made me want to rip open his head but...I couldn't. I should be happy that I couldn't...right? I went back to join everyone in the living room.

"We are not done trading presents. There is one more present that needs to be opened," Olivia said four boxes coming from behind her.

"Did you know she had those over there?" Beauti said her breath hot on my ear.

"No," I reply. She shrugged. Olivia softly threw one box in front of Cole, Beauti, Bella and then me. We all looked at the boxes in front of us and opened them. Inside was a white shirt saying in big black words, *FRIENDS COME AND GO* on the front but on the back it said, *BUT FAMILY IS FOR FOREVER AND BEYOND.* I looked at Bella's shirt and she had the same one. So did Cole and Beauti.

"This is our new family shirt," Olivia said.

"You guys have one too?" Cole asked.

"Yes. And we are wearing it today for Christmas!" Daddy said checking out his shirt. I looked at Beauti and she didn't look so happy. I mean, this is just a little much, but when you have parents, we couldn't do anything. We just had to go with the flow.

»»»

"I hate this shirt, okay?" Beauti said tugging at the new "family shirt." I don't like it either but what can I do?

We were getting dressed for Christmas dinner. Almost every one of my family members were coming tonight. They come every year unless someone gets sick or something like that. And Olivia forced us all to wear her new t-shirts she got us.

"How do I look? Good? Hmm?" Bella said her ponytail high on her head and her black letters matching her black leggings.

"You look good," I said.

"Thank you. Thank you...I try," she said raising her eyebrows. She went into the bathroom and I followed her. We saw Beauti putting on...makeup?

"You wear makeup?" I asked hands on my hips.

"No, I just wear the mascara and lip gloss. Sometimes, Mom let's me wear real makeup," she said. I nodded my head understanding.

"Do you think she'll let me wear makeup?" I asked.

"To be honest, maybe she'll just let you wear lip gloss. Mascara and that stuff, I'm not so sure," Beauti said and then brushed the mascara on her eyelashes. Well, I don't even know how to work it so maybe it's not necessary.

Kat started wearing makeup this year. I noticed on the first day of school that she was wearing mascara, lipstick, and her eyelids were colored. She also had on blush that blended with her skin. Daddy certainly would not let me wear that to school...or anywhere right now.

"Knock, knock," Olivia said coming in. We all said come in at the same time. She was wearing her shirt with black jeans instead of leggings like us.

"Hi, Mom," Beauti smiled.

"Hi, girls. Anyone excited to meet Alyssa's family?"

Olivia said. Bella raised her hand as soon as Olivia stopped talking. Beauti raised her hand but shook it back and forth.

"I can't wait, but I'm nervous," Beauti said.

"Oh don't be!" I chirped, "you will love my family. Especially, Grandma Lyla. She is SO awesome! Best grandma ever!"

"I don't know your grandma, but Beauti and I have the best grandma. Which is obviously, Nana," Bella said sitting down on the lid of the toilet. I didn't argue. Everyone thinks their grandma is the best so...yeah.

"Whatever, but you'll also like Norris. He's my cousin. His older sister, Noelle, is a little..." I tried to look for the words.

"Brat?" Beauti asked.

"Beauti!" Olivia gave her a glare.

"Yes. She is. She's so...she's just such a teenager!" I said thinking about Noelle on her phone and never really speaking to anyone.

"Alyssa, don't talk about people like that," Olivia said. "Even if they are," she finishes. Beauti looked at me and snickered a little. We all went out of the bathroom ready to start Christmas Dinner.

»»»

Cole and I were having a game of thumb war when the doorbell rang. Beauti was on her phone and Bella was....where was she? Cole lets go of my hand and went to open the door.

"If you touch that door, I will make sure you are grounded," Daddy said coming down the stairs. I laughed a little. Cole knew he was not supposed to open the door for nobody!

He sighed unhappily but stayed near the door waiting to see who was here first. By looking at her gray coat, I knew who she was before I saw her face.

"Grandma Lyla!" I said going to give her a hug. She wrapped her arms around me.

"I missed you, Alyssa," she said kissing my head.

"I missed you too," I said. Then she looked around to find Cole. He was standing there but then rushed into her arms.

Cole might be a pain in the butt, but he does love someone very fiercely. I watched them hug each other, and then Olivia showed up. She stood next to Daddy. Her face seemed nervous, and you could see the small sweat beads on the side of her head.

Grandma Lyla let go of Cole, to look at Olivia.

"You must be, Olivia. Joseph has told me a lot about you," Grandma Lyla said shaking Olivia's hand.

"Yes, I am. I hope he told you nice things about me," Olivia said returning the handshake.

"Yes, he did! I'm just happy he found love again, after my daughter," Grandma Lyla said coming inside and sitting down on one of the chairs. At first, Olivia looked confused.

"You're Kara's mom?" Olivia asked.

"Yes. And I am happy Joseph chose you. And I want to talk to you in private," Grandma Lyla said taking her arm. She mouthed bye to all of us as Grandma Lyla dragged her away.

Right when they left, the doorbell rang again. Aunt Jasmine and Uncle Lloyd were here. Behind them was Noelle on her phone and Norris just standing there. Laughter filled the house as they came in. Uncle Lloyd is Dad's older brother. My mom had only brothers.

"Oh, Alyssa look how tall you are!" Aunt Jasmine screamed in excitement as she picked me up, my nose digging into her blondish brownish hair. It smelled good.

"Hi Aunt Jaz," I said. I gave her a kiss on her cheeks.

"How are you?"

"Good."

"Have any boyfriends?" She asked raising her eyebrows up and down. My cheeks became hotter than the sun itself.

"Ew, no!" I said. Aunt Jasmine laughed.

"I was kidding. Your father would kill you and the boyfriend," she said. I smiled because that was the truth. Then I looked up at, Uncle Lloyd.

"Hi," I said to him.

"Come here, Big-Head!" Uncle Lloyd smiled shaking and hugging me to death. I couldn"t believe he still called me

Big-Head. When I was born, he gave me that nickname 'cause he thought my head was big, and he never called me by my real name, unless it was serious.

He let me go. Daddy told them about Olivia and then he called Bella and Beauti to come meet them. Bella was still happy and cheerful, but you could see that Beauti was shy, like the first time I met her. She kept looking at Noelle too, but the brat barely even picked up her head. I felt like slapping her for being so rude.

»»»

I was getting bored listening to Norris' breakup stories about all the girls that broke his heart. Like, do I care if his ex-girlfriend, Dori, or whatever her name was, dumped him? The answer was no! Yes, it probably hurts to get dumped but like, he's fourteen years old. And telling me was bad because I was only eleven! When he got a call, I decided that was my opportunity to leave.

I went upstairs to see if Grandma Lyla and Olivia were done talking. But I heard their voices and they were not done.

"Alyssa is in pain. Anyone that looks at her can tell. But you can give her hope again," I heard Grandma Lyla say. She took Olivia's hand in hers.

"You can give her hope about love, now that her mother's gone, but still in our hearts. You can be the new mother for her, like Kara. She needs it! Joseph can't do it alone," she said.

"I will be here for her. I'll claim Alyssa Halse as mine. She's my daughter now," Olivia said. Grandma Lyla smiled.

"Yes, she is. And do the things I told you to do with her. The things she missed most about her mom, okay?"

"I will," Olivia said getting off the bed coming towards the door. I started to panic. What was I going to do? If Olivia saw me here, she' would think that I was eavesdropping on her. And I was but...ugh!

I pretended to act like I was going to the bathroom right when Olivia came out. A smile arose on her face.

"Well, hello Alyssa," she said.

"Hi," I said. I continued with my plan and went into the bathroom. I turned the light on and waited. When I was positive that Olivia was downstairs, I went out of the bathroom to find Grandma Lyla standing right there.

"Whoa, wow!" I said waving my hand over my face, "you don't want to go in there. It smelled pretty bad," I finished holding my nose. Even if I had to embarass myself, this had to be done. Grandma Lyla laughed. She'd bought it.

"This is Alyssa and Cole's grandma girls," Olivia said coming up the stairs, followed by Beauti and Bella...and Cole. Grandma Lyla looked at them and smiled.

"You girls are gorgeous," she said giving them a hug.

"Especially you, Beauti. No wonder you were named Beauti," Grandma Lyla said. I smiled. Happy that she liked them, but couldn't help the pang of jealousy that came when she complimented Beauti on her face. And you could see that Beauti liked the compliment and she was blushing. Not just on her cheeks, but her whole face was redder than a strawberry.

»»»

"Your grandma is so fun!" Bella said. We had been hanging out with Grandma Lyla all Christmas dinner. She was leaving in a few minutes.

"Well, she is not just my grandma anymore she's-"

"She's never been just your grandma, Alyssa. She's mine too!" Cole interrupted me.

I rolled my eyes. "Yes, she's not just my grandma. She belongs to me and Cole but-"

"But not anymore! She's Bella and Beauti's too."

"Cole just shut up!" I yelled at him. He got very quiet.

"Sorry, but you interrupted me. So, I got mad," I said breathing in and out.

"Yeah, why'd you think I did it?" Cole said and I launched myself at him but Daddy came in and stopped me.

"It's never time to kill each other, okay?" Daddy said. I sighed like I was upset but then sat back down.

"It's time to say goodbye to Grandma Lyla," he said to all of us. Cole and I rushed down. We had this thing about when Grandma Lyla let our house, we would always have a race to see who could get a hug from her first. Cole won today.

I gave Grandma Lyla a hug, and said goodbye. She told me that I was lucky, that my dad had found Olivia. I told her I was thankful. She told me and Cole, that she knew we're moving. Olivia had already given her the address. She said bye to Beauti and Bella too.

»»»

"Well girls, goodnight," Olivia said tucking in Bella and then giving Beauti a kiss on the head. She came over to me and gave me a kiss too. I told her goodnight.

"When are we going to start packing for the move?" I asked before Olivia completely disappeared. She turned around to look at me.

"Your dad wants to start packing you guys up tomorrow. He wants to move as soon as possible," she said. I nodded my head.

"Don't worry, okay? The move will be fine. Yes, you'll miss your friends but-."

"No, I'm not worried. I was just thinking. I want to move away," I interrupted her. She nodded her head. I could tell she wanted to say something else but held it back on a tight leash. I guessed there was still a little hesitation between me and her. But every day, our relationship would improve. That's good. I shut my eyes trying to dream of Olivia's house. Where I'll now be living. New school, New...friends. New...I drifted off.

~6~

Two Months Later.

I walked home from school with Beauti, her friends, Lana and Amanda. Okay, let me backtrack.

I now go to Bieber-Creek Middle School with Beauti. We live so close that we walk to school. I can bring my phone because Olivia wants us to be okay. I tried calling Olivia--Mom--a few times but it sounded awkward and weird. But step by step, I'll get there.

Cole and Bella go to the same elementary school, so they get dropped off and picked up by Olivia and Daddy. They get home first before Beauti and I.

I've grown to like Beauti's friends even though they ignore me at times. But it's okay because I made new friends. I haven't forgotten about Kat, but I've stopped thinking about her. I mean, she didn't really care that I was moving, and we wouldn't be in the same school anymore, but she and I will go to the same high school. Again, she didn't care.

My new friends are pretty cool, though. I have made a lot of them in a short period of time, but the ones I'm really close to are Rowan, Sharia, and Maura.

Rowan is very funny, and she has the loveliest face. Whenever I see her, I can't help but get lost into her huge chocolaty brown eyes and her shoulder length brown hair is even more attractive. And then Sharia's bright ginger red hair could almost blind you. Her seaweed green eyes and full face of freckles will attract you too, and you won't be able to look away. Last but not least, Maura. Oh, Maura. She is so silly, that you just...can't keep your guard up. She might look like a shy girl with her big, square, maroon glasses, but no! She's so lively. I'm so glad I can call them my friends. I didn't tell them about my mom dying. I don't want them to pity me. I don't want them to feel sorry. So, they don't know that piece about me.

»»»

"Hey, you okay?" Beauti nudged me. I looked up at her blue eyes.

"Oh, yeah. I'm just lost in thought," I said. She nodded and then we walked up to the porch parting away from Lana and Amanda. Olivia's house was bigger than our old one. I still have my own room, and so did Beauti and Bella. Cole slept by himself too. I liked how my life was going so far

"You have the key right?" I asked Beauti. She snaked around in her pocket, trying to find the keys. Her face turned red as she muttered angrily. I shook my head laughing a little.

"You don't do you?"

"Nope," she said. I snickered a little.

"And you're supposed to be the older and 'responsible' one," I said getting my own keys from my book bag. Beauti smiled.

"I can't do all the work all the time," she said as the door squeaked open, "I have three siblings to look after now. Not just one annoying one, but three!" She said. I didn't realize at first that she basically just classified me as annoying.

"Hey!" I softly elbowed her in her ribs. She laughed and so did I.

Changes

"Well, hello there girls," Olivia said coming towards us. Beauti and I said hi at the same time.

"How was school?" Daddy said coming from the living room, popcorn in his hands.

"Good," I said.

"Normal," Beauti replied. I shook my head at Beauti. That's been her reply lately whenever Olivia and Dad asked how was school.

Bella and Cole came running too, sliding on the marble floor because of their socks. In order to anchor himself, Cole grabbed my shirt and he and I both went down. Pain shot through my butt. Let me just tell you... ow! I looked at him giving him the worst glare ever.

"Sorry. I just wanted to say that tonight's Friday Family Night," he said scratching his hair in embarrassment. I rolled my eyes as I worked myself back onto my feet.

"Don't you think I know that, Dork!?" I yelled a little.

"Alyssa calm down. He said sorry," Olivia said putting a hand on my shoulder. I sighed. If Mom and Dad weren't here I would've made him go through the pain, my butt had faced a few seconds ago.

"Come on. The movie's about to start!" Bella said tugging on Daddy. He followed her to the family room and so did we. I lay my book bag down and put my phone on silent, as I got a text from Rowan, Sharia, and Maura.

Rowan: Is tonight ur family night? If it is, call me tomorrow. Bye.

I quickly texted back and went to sit next to Mom. Time for a movie.

My life had changed in just a few months. It wasn't a small change, but it was HUGE. And honestly, I didn't think I would like it. I thought I would hate it, more than hating losing my mom, but, look at me now. I have a new mom who is just the best, two new siblings that are not so annoying like Cole, and then it's just perfect. Change, I've found out, isn't so bad after all. So, don't be afraid of it. Embrace it.

"I love you guys!" I said before the movie started.

"Shush!" They all replied. I laughed. My new family! My new change.

Message from the Author

My Autobiography

My name is Mahawa Bangoura. I am currently twelve years old. I was born in Conakry, Guinea, West Africa. I am the baby and the only girl of four children in my new family. In order to prepare me to live in America, with my new family, my father and his new wife took me to The Gambia. It is the smallest country in Africa and its official language is English. There I went to a private school where I learned English because the only language I knew was my native language, Sous sous. At the age of five, I started to speak American English.

In February 2012, I came to the United States with my father and my youngest brother to join my new mother and my two new brothers. My new mother decided that it would be best for me to be placed in first grade instead of second grade. I had no concept of the American education system and my English needed improvement. Therefore, I attended ESL (English as a Second Language) for a year and a half. I now attend a Middle School in New Jersey.

Changes

My love for writing began when my new mother and I would tell each other stories. I loved to exchange stories back and forth, and listening to them had my undivided attention. The stories she told me, piqued my imagination. They made me want to continue telling stories in my own words and in my own way. That's when I knew I could tell stories and make them whatever I wanted them to be and the thought of that made me so happy.

In third grade, I began to love reading. I read books and fell in love with the characters, the plot, and just the whole idea of books. When I wrote my own books, I felt enormously happy. I wanted to write books that people could read, and fall in love with the characters just like I did. I liked the idea of people everywhere reading my books and not wanting to put them down until every single page had been read. I have written four books, and one is still in the process.

Reading and writing is very important to me, I wrote my first book at age nine when I realized that I enjoyed writing so much.

Mahawa Bangoura

Changes